To Shirley
Best Wishes
Mikkan

MIKE AND A LYNX

NAMED KITTY

Second Edition

MIKE AND A LYNX

NAMED KITTY

Second Edition

By

Mike Kerr

Illustrations by
Karren Vitt

PUBLISHING

iv

First Edition printed 2003
Second Edition printed 2006

Published by:
KiwE Publishing, Ltd.
Spokane, WA
http://www.kiwepublishing.com

Library of Congress Control Number: 2006929670

ISBN-10 1-931195-36-6
ISBN-13 978-1-931195-36-2

Edited by Valle Novak
Thomas Buchanan, Literary Advisor
Illustrations by Karren Vitt

Printed in the United States of America

Dedicated to the memory of

Merry E. DeBord,

loving wife and mother

and faithful friend.

ACKNOWLEDGMENT

*Special acknowledgment and gratitude
goes to two photographers whose
photographs were indispensable in
creating the drawings for this book.
First, Nancy Vandermey of the
EFBC's Feline Conservation Center
(located in Rosamond, California) for
her wonderful photographs of Trapper,
a young male Canadian Lynx,
and second, Margaret Hunter
of Cat Tales in Mead, Washington,
for sending photos of Tasha,
their mature female Canadian Lynx.*

viii

ABOUT THE AUTHOR

Michael Kerr was born and raised on Kodiak Island, Alaska. The son of a Danish fisherman and a native Alaskan mother, his youth was filled with the adventures of which he writes.

He fished commercially with his father and brother in the 1930s and '40s, learned to fly as a youngster and was licensed as a private pilot when he joined the US Air Force during the Korean War. Upon discharge, he married, fathered eight children and after losing his beloved wife, Merry, decided to write a fictional children's story based on his real-life childhood adventures.

INTRODUCTION

This story is set in the small villages and towns in Alaska. From olden days right up to the 1940's, boys were taught at an early age about survival and occupational skills to prepare them for a life of hard work.

The main occupation was commercial fishing, with trapping and hunting both as income sources and for food on the table. Boys began these endeavors around the age of five or six, and girls were taught homemaking skills, gardening, and later, after age 12 or so, often worked in fish canning factories.

Commercial fishing for salmon was done by purse seining or gill netting.

In purse seining, the net was piled on the stern of the fishing boat and one end hooked to a skiff. When the net was released, the boat would make a large circle around and back to the skiff bringing the two net ends together. The nets were 150 to 200 fathoms, six feet to a fathom. The bottom of the net was weighted down with lead sinkers, about three pounds per foot. The top was floated with corks, about $3^1/_2$ pounds per foot. When the boats met, the leads were drawn up forming a bag or "purse" full of fish. All of this was done by hand.

With gill netting, the net was anchored to land and stretched out in the water by a skiff in a straight line with the outer end formed into a triangle. Upon coming to the net, fish would follow it along, looking for an opening and were literally "herded" into the triangular trap from which they could not escape.

Most families lived off the land and from the sea: seafood, rabbits, moose, and caribou were the most common fare. Gardens were planted for vegetables such as potatoes, carrots, turnips, cabbages, and other hardy crops. Boys and girls both were taught to hunt and by the time they were around eight years old were excellent shots.

Most children were bi- or tri-lingual, using their native language, plus Russian and English. If the father was Scandinavian, they learned that as well. Generally, in the home the parent's language was spoken, but outside the home English was used.

LYNX

There are two types of lynx in the far north: Canadian and Siberian. The Siberian is found mostly in Alaska. Lynx grow to about three feet in length and some 30 inches at the shoulder. They have large round paws that adapt to the snow, on which they spread out like snowshoes.

Lynx are not ready for mating or reproduction until about two years old. In the wild a lynx will live for more than 15 years; in captivity, over 21 years. The lynx adapts well to domestication, especially within its own environment.

The lynx is very much at home in the cold northern forests and its coat of thick short, brown-gray fur not only keeps it warm, but merges with the background of mosses and lichens on the forest floor. The lynx that range in the Alaskan forests are mostly spotted. With its big, softly furred feet, the lynx is able to move silently through the forest as it stalks its prey, primarily snowshoe rabbit. With their keen sense of hearing and smell, they can locate rodents under the snow and in darkness.

A very adaptable cat, lynx are excellent swimmers and ferocious fighters in the water. On land, a lynx can jump from a standstill to over eight feet straight up.

Lynx have very few enemies in the wild because of their speed and extreme strength. They have been known to break a wolf's neck with one powerful blow of their front paws. Their only real enemy is man, who has always sought their beautiful and valuable fur.

ONE

Spring had come to the Alaskan island. The sun warmed the earth, and glistened on the emerald green waters of the bay that lay along the quiet small town. The lava rocks on the beach looked like polished black onyx in the receding tide. A variety of sea birds swam slowly at the edge of the bay, completing the picture of beauty and serenity.

It was a peaceful home for young Mike, an outdoorsman in the making; bright, spry and an adventurer. His only fault was a quick tongue when he knew he was right. Many times his mother exiled him to a forest encampment. He usually was glad to leave and be on his own, for when his father was away her patience ran thin. Mike had made the lean-to and campsite with the supervision of his father when he was five years old. It was constructed of large spruce limbs laid upon a frame of long poles so that it would be solid for years to come. The fireplace was raked clear of all debris so as not to make a hazard of forest fire. It was then surrounded by smooth river stones brought up from a creek located about a half mile away.

Although it was early May, the hill behind the town was turning a lush green. The alder, cottonwood and birch trees were sprouting young leaves. The hill looked like a jade sculpture dotted with emeralds. The streams and brooks that flowed through town sparked like diamonds, rejoicing in their rebirth after a long harsh winter.

In the small town on the island, the boy and his family lived in the traditional setting of a fishing and trapping community. They lived a simple life with the combined influences of the native and Russian cultures. Mike was born to a father from Denmark who had moved to the island and married a native woman of high standard. It was her wish to raise their children to serve as priests and be well grounded in the Russian Orthodox Church. Their lives were very basic and had only a few events to change this. The fishing companies had financed many fishing boats and "Big Mike" was one of them. This was the family's first source of income. Trapping was the

second. The town was in transition as a new military base was being built close by. Many new people and ideas showed up as well. The town was growing very rapidly.

The previous year was not too successful for many fishermen, Big Mike included. They worked long seasons to catch the salmon and bring them to the cannery. Many fathers started teaching their sons to fish at six years of age. Young Mike had stayed home while others his age went. He never asked why, he just thought that his father didn't want him along.

Mike sat on a flat rock by a man-made pool on the stream that flowed by his home. This was one of Mike's favorite places for it was within earshot of the house yet out of his mother's way. The preparations for the up-coming fishing season were in full swing. As he sat there with chin cradled in his knees, looking at the glimmering water in the early sun, he felt a loneliness and confusion as he contemplated on the past year.

Young Mike, soon to be ten, had worked in his father's blacksmith shop for the last two years. Big Mike was a large man with strong features. His face was reddish from the wind and salt spray. His lips were straight and never seemed to smile. His eyes were steel blue, with a gaze that could seemingly stop a charging grizzly bear in its tracks. With wisdom from a hard life of hunting, fishing, and many years on the wilderness frontier, he had a hard look about his face. He was a man of few words and stood tall in Mike's eyes.

Mike had worked hard for the past winter after school and on Saturdays. He was paid five cents an hour. He could have made more money if he had been allowed to fish with his father.

Resentment was welling up inside him as he thought of the fall before when he and his father had gone to a nearby island to hunt. On the way back to town without warning they hit a sunken log. The waves were three to four feet high but were not white-capping. The boat was sinking fast. Young Mike scrambled to launch the dory as his father hurried to grab a rifle and some provisions. As young Mike jumped into the dory, a wave caught his left foot between the dory and the boat. He wrenched with pain as he heard, more than felt the bones in his foot snap.

He held on to the boat while his father jumped into the dory. They both pushed the dory away from the boat with an oar just as the cabin of the boat went under. The boat was completely lost and they were on their own, since they were not expected home for another week.

As they rowed to shore, young Mike huddled in the bow of the dory. As they hit the beach he jumped up, putting pressure on the foot. The excruciating pain caused him to fall overboard.

Mike slipped into the surf head first. His father grabbed him and heaved him onto the beach. "What

are you doing Mike, can't you walk on the legs?"
Young Mike told his father how his foot had gotten
caught between the skiff and the boat. Big Mike
then took hold of Mike's boot to pull it off. He
yanked roughly, young Mike turned white from
the pain and almost fainted. The foot was too
swollen to remove the boot. It was then his father
took his hunting knife and cut the boot and sock
off. The foot was turning black and was bent at an
odd angle at the arch. His father gave him some
matches and told him to crawl up on the beach
near a pile of driftwood and build a fire; which he
painfully did, leaving Big Mike on the beach.

In a short while his father returned with some
clay, tree bark and twine he made from the bow
rope on the dory. As his father grabbed the foot
and jerked on it, young Mike fainted. When he

awoke his foot was propped up on some round smooth rocks by the fire in a cast of river clay and tree bark. Together they built a lean-to and Mike hobbled around gathering firewood.

As time passed, the weather turned bad and it rained very heavily. On the third day it started to snow, "It's time we start walking Mike, for they aren't going to look for us until late in the season," Big Mike stated. "The trip is going to be rough and hard so brace yourself. We have to go over the mountains to the nearest town."

It was more than forty miles to the town and over some very rough terrain. Mike walked the whole distance with a broken foot using a driftwood crutch to keep the weight off the foot.

It seemed a lifetime had passed as they finally topped the ridge overlooking the houses of the small town. When they arrived the foot was seen by a doctor and placed in a new cast of plaster.

The doctor was impressed: "From the looks of the exams, you did a good job resetting the bones, Big Mike."

"I had no choice to save his foot from being sideways the rest of his life Doc," his father replied with a slight curve to his lips. While the doctor was finishing up with young Mike, his father made arrangements to get them home. Once there, all Mike's mother would say was, "I don't want my son to be lost on your choice of life."

As Mike sat and thought on these things he heard his father calling, "Mike, I need you to come inside now, I have to talk to you."

When he went inside his father and mother were sitting at the kitchen table. His father announced,

"I will be taking you to the fishing grounds this season to help take care of the camp."

His mother protested, "Mike will miss his services at the Mission. It was agreed that he will stay home to help me with the things around the house. If something happens to you both I will be all alone. I have lost too much already," Mike's mother pleaded.

"If we continue to do this he will not be able to learn to fish. It is not a good thing to shelter a boy so," Big Mike explained. It was then that Mike knew why he never went fishing with his father. A pride welled up in him as he realized his father had not rejected him and wanted him to go.

"Mike, get yourself some clothes together and I'll see you in the kitchen in a half-hour," his father instructed.

"Okay, I'll be ready."

Mike flew into his room gathering things he knew he was going to need. As he moved in a silent manner he thought about his mother and hoped she wouldn't be too upset, for the season lasted three to four months. As he carried his bedroll and pack into the kitchen he checked off the supply list.

After all the packing, the list was gone over, and young Mike, his father and his father's native partner Cappy, met at the dock. Cappy piped out "What are we supposed to do with the boy, Big Mike?"

"We aren't doing anything, he is coming along to keep camp this year and help with chores so we can catch more fish."

"I like to see that," said Cappy in his broken English; "he can't do much, he too small."

Big Mike answered, "He can hunt and cook and clean up after meals, saving us valuable time and if you don't like it then find another partner." The discussion was closed.

Big Mike started looking over the boat and nets. "We have a lot to do before we head out now, so let's stop talking and get busy."

"Father, I can help, just let me know what to do." Mike spoke quietly, so as not to be heard by Cappy.

"Mike can paint and repair dories and the skiff and do net repairs," Big Mike told Cappy.

They started by unloading the nets, dories and the skiff. "Mike you are to patch, sand and paint the boats tomorrow, we will get you on the nets as soon as you finish." That evening Mike and his father returned to the house late. Both father and son were tired; they ate, and then went to bed.

Morning came early at 5:30 A.M. The smell of sourdough pancakes wafted throughout the home. His mother called at the bedroom door: "Mike, time to get up. I have your food ready in five minutes,"

"Okay, I'll be right there, mother." Mike rolled out of his warm bed and headed for the clothes he wore the day before. As he dressed he thought, "I will show Cappy that I'm the best helper he and father ever thought of having." He finished up with the boots his father had to buy last fall and remembered to make his bed.

Sitting down at the table he greeted his father. "Good day to paint and get those boats finished, isn't it father?"

"Yes it is," said Big Mike. "I have to buy new corks and weights for the nets; the others aren't any good. I suppose you can put them on for me after the paint."

"I need you to show me how they'll be done," Mike said as he was the partner instead of a son.

After breakfast was finished they prepared a lunch for noon then left to the dock for the day. As they approached the docks Cappy joined them. "Morning, Big Mike. I was thinking about servicing the motor and getting the ropes ready on the boat today. What do you think?" Cappy asked.

"Well that sounds great. I need to go to the store and get the corks and weights for the nets later this afternoon."

"Will you pick out some more rope? I need about 180 feet," Cappy requested.

"Sure, if you think of anything else let me know."

Big Mike walked over to the dories and was looking at how much work was to be done. "Mike, you are to fill the scrapes and sand them when dry. Then seal the whole bottom of each of them. Got it?"

Mike spoke up, "I'll do my best, father," as he gathered his tools for the job and started in on the first boat.

In a few days, the work was done and after bidding farewell to Mike's mother, they set off to the fishing grounds on the mainland. As they came in, they saw the fishing barge near the cove designated to store their catch. The catch was to be tallied as the cannery tender collected catches from the barge biweekly. Cappy and Big Mike took a moment to see that the barge was secure and placed extra supplies on it then proceeded to their base camp.

The fish camp was in a sheltered cove with a long crescent-shaped sandy beach. A crystal clear stream flowed about fifty feet from the cabin which was actually a wooden frame covered by a canvas tent. There was a homemade stove and a hand made table. Tree stumps were used for chairs. The camp was surrounded on three sides by mountains.

Once the boat was anchored, the dory was rowed repeatedly to and from shore to unload the season's supplies for camp. Everything was stored in an orderly state. To keep organized was an important standard for Big Mike. He had assured his son that organization is a necessity in the life of a fisherman. You use it, and then put it in its proper place. That was the general rule.

TWO

———>●<———

One day the two men told young Mike that he would have to stay in camp and watch the beans and ham hocks they had started cooking for supper that night. As he sat there on a log not far from the tent he thought he heard something by the stream that sounded like a kitten.

On investigating, he found a lynx kitten; it seemed very weak. The looks of the cub told Mike that it needed food, so he took it back to camp.

He mixed some milk and water and tried to get the kitten to drink out of a bowl. Kitty (as young Mike named it) would lick milk off his finger, so he first put some milk on his finger and enticed Kitty to the bowl, and then placed his finger in the bowl leading Kitty to the milk. After getting a few snoots full of milk he learned to drink from the bowl. Mike placed the kitten in a bed made from his dirty clothes. It slept most of the afternoon.

That night when the two men returned to camp, Mike called excitedly, "Dad I have to show you what I found today!" He was anxious to show his father the cub.

"Mike, you are not to take wild animals to camp, home, or any place else. You should not have touched it either," Big Mike scolded. "I have seen a family of lynx up the ridge next to the stream."

His father took the cub and rubbed it with seaweed and dirt. Then he wrapped it in seaweed and told young Mike to carry it that way and not to touch it with his bare hands. He explained, "Its mother may not accept it if she smells human scent on it."

Mike headed to the den's destination with the muddy seaweed ball of fur in his arms, doing exactly as instructed, for even he knew that his father was right. The cub had to be returned to be raised in his own environment.

Not far from the camp they came upon a huge freshly downed dead tree. As they were passing Mike had spotted a muff of fur under the tree. They investigated, and sadly found the mother lynx and a sister crushed to death under the deadfall. Mike's father looked at him and said, "We can't let the cub starve."

"What can we do with him?" Mike asked.

"We'll take him back to camp and help him a little, son." As they started to leave Mike said to his father "It isn't right to leave his family like that. We should bury them." Mike expected a protest from his father. He was pleasantly surprised when his father replied, "Yes, you go to camp and get the shovel and axe and I'll try to remove them from under the deadfall."

Mike placed Kitty back at camp. When he returned, he found his father busy and digging with a limb of a tree what would be the two lynx graves. Together they finished a deep hole and placed the cats to rest following up with large stones and dirt to secure the resting place of Kitty's family. Mike turned around and found Kitty sitting there on a log watching as they finished up. Mike then picked him up and cradled him in his arms knowing Kitty realized he was alone without a family. "I guess that I'll be your family now," Mike said to the kitten. The lynx meowed as if replying to Mike's statement.

As they walked back to camp, Mike was observing his father. At one point, his father turned and looked at Mike and Kitty. Mike thought he detected a gleam in his father's eyes and a faint smile. It may have been the first time Mike had gained his father's respect for his love of nature and caring for animals that inspired the look of satisfaction on his father's face.

Mike had the extra responsibility to watch the kitten as it was growing during the next few months. His father told him, "If the lynx does any damage it is up to you to take care of it. I will not have a wild animal caged or tied up and it must learn to take care of itself." Mike vigorously nodded his agreement, "Yes father I will do everything you've asked." Mike was bound and determined to show his father he would do what was expected of him.

The next morning, Mike ate, fed Kitty, and then asked "is it all right if I take a hike to the cave to see where he was born, father?" His father thought for a moment and said, "Mike, you know that you have to take care of camp today, I guess it won't hurt, just be back before dark."

"I plan to leave after the dishes are done and the firewood is stacked up," Mike replied.

Finishing his chores, Mike headed to the spring and up the canyon with Kitty he went. The stream was fast, running five to six feet across, and was in places four to five feet deep with some large stones at the edges big enough to sit and rest on. The banks were filled with brush and berry bushes that made it difficult to manage a path at times. As they crossed the deadfall, he noticed Kitty sniffing the remaining scent of the family he had lost. Mike's thoughts turned to sympathy for the lone cat. He decided that cats have feelings as people do. They left after a few minutes so they could be back to camp in time to make dinner. It was about two miles to the den from camp.

The rest of the summer passed quickly. Kitty grew quite large. He was hunting a little, catching a few mice around camp and an occasional snowshoe rabbit. Mike's father let Mike know frequently that the lynx was his responsibility. As the season ended, Mike's father consented to taking Kitty back to town with them.

THREE

As fall progressed, Kitty and Mike took many hunting trips into the woods outside of town. Kitty learned to hunt for himself. It was a mild winter that year and the rabbits were plentiful. This made for a well-fed lynx. Kitty lived under the roots of a tree in the yard of Mike's home. It was the perfect home for the cat.

Spring arrived and the two men, the boy, and the lynx returned to the fishing camp. Kitty recognized his birth home and would disappear for days but would always return to camp. Kitty loved going out on the boat with the men. He would spend a lot of time around camp. At the end of the season they returned to town. Again Kitty returned with them. He was now full grown and the family ran into a lot of opposition from the newcomers about having a wild lynx in town with no restraints.

There was an older lawyer that moved to town. He was mean-spirited and disliked by most of the people in town, including natives and newcomers alike. He raised Dobermans. The dogs were taught to be mean and ill tempered. The lawyer would walk the dogs on long leashes and corner the kids, letting the dogs lunge at the children, allowing them to come within inches of their bodies.

A new girl, named Leatha, had moved to town. She had long blonde hair like spun gold and bright blue eyes that were always smiling.One day the old lawyer had her pinned against a building with one of his dogs, letting it lunge at her. As the dog gave a ferocious lunge, the leash broke. Mike and Kitty were a couple of blocks away. Kitty heard the commotion and took off like a streak of lightning, hitting the dog broadside and knocking it over and off the girl. Before the dog could regain its footing Kitty was on him again. Kitty stood on his hind legs like a grizzly bear and with one powerful swing of his forepaw

broke the dog's neck. He then went over to Leatha and stood by her protectively. It wasn't until Mike arrived on the scene that Kitty would let anyone near the girl. The public health nurse was soon on the scene. She and one of the elders and a newcomer were putting Leatha in a vehicle when she cried, "Bring Kitty, bring Kitty." So Mike and Kitty went to the hospital with her.

Mike and Kitty waited while Leatha was in the operating room. When she was moved into a recovery room Mike and Kitty were allowed to visit. Kitty stood on his hind legs and put his front paws on the bed, resting his head on them. Leatha stroked him behind the ears. It was the first time Kitty let anybody except Mike touch him, Mike told Leatha.

"He sure is beautiful, where did you get him?" Leatha asked.

Mike told her the story: "I found him at the fishing camp. His family was killed by a deadfall the wind blew down. He was the only one that made it," Mike explained.

Leatha's father and mother worked at the
military base so it took them a while to get to the
hospital. Just as Mike and Kitty were leaving they
walked by. Her father muttered, "Damn native and
his wild cat." Then Mike heard Leatha say, "Dad,
if it was not for that damn native, as you call him,
and his cat, I'd be dead." The public health nurse
explained to them how the old lawyer was teasing
her with one of his dogs when the leash broke and
the dog attacked her, biting her on the face, neck
and shoulders when Kitty intervened and killed the
dog, and that it was at Leatha's request that they
were there. This was the beginning of a new and
better relationship between the newcomers and
natives.

As Mike walked toward home he thought about
how harshly Leatha had spoken to her father. This

was unheard of amongst the town people. As they were walking, a young newcomer stopped them and told Mike that the old lawyer had gone home and released all his dogs. As a passing motorist watched in horror, the dogs attacked and killed the lawyer. When help arrived it was too late and the dogs all were eliminated before they could do any more damage.

When Mike and Kitty got home he thought his father had a smile on his face. Mike asked his parents if he could go to his camp for a few days His mother started to protest but his father interrupted; finally they agreed to let him go.

As Mike was getting his things ready, his father walked in and took Mike's old single shot .22 and handed him a brand new lever-action .22 rifle. To Mike it was like a gold medal. It was the first and last thing of material value that he would receive from his father.

Mike and Kitty walked up the hill and turned northwest toward a stand of spruce trees. As they walked through the forest, a thick carpet of moss cushioned their footsteps. They soon came to a beaver pond that was frozen over. Mike started across the pond when Kitty squatted and arched his back. Mike took a large rock and tossed it onto the ice to see it disappear under the deep water. Kitty had known the ice was not safe in the center of the pond so they traveled on the perimeter until they reached the beaver dam and crossed there. They followed the stream for a while, and then turned to walk along the edge line of the spruce trees. Below them was a small valley covered with cottonwood and alder trees that went down to the

waters edge. It was a U-shaped bay with very little beach. At one side was the mountain with high cliffs jutting up over the water. The other side was a point of land that stuck out into the water; below was a reef that had surfaced to be seen above the waterline.

Mike had used this place, at the point in the spruce trees, many times previously. A lake fed the stream close by. His lean-to and fireplace he had built on earlier visits made it easier for him to settle in. Mike proceeded to clean his ashes from the stone-circled fireplace and prepared new forked sticks to place his food on to cook. He collected new boughs of spruce to cover his lean-to, gathered firewood consisting of some green alders and cottonwood to make a bed of coals for cooking. As Mike prepared to eat some smoked salmon,

Kitty returned to camp, so Mike gave Kitty some as well. They feasted on hardtack and tea to complete their meal.

After the meal, Kitty trotted back to the woods. Mike walked out to the point that overlooked the ocean bay. The point looked quite bare since the grass had turned golden as the season changed. Mike approached the end of the point to see snow-capped mountains of the mainland. This was a peaceful place that Mike had enjoyed many times during the years. The water in the bay was calm as a sheet of glass. He noticed two humpback whales surfacing in the distance; they glided lazily, blowing as they resurfaced, then quietly sinking out of sight. It was late for the whales to be so far north.

Looking out over the beauty and stillness Mike's thoughts drifted to the young Leatha in the hospital

and how she was very defiant in her defense of Kitty and himself. How that night her father came to the house and thanked him. He thought about spring and fishing with his father even when his mother protested. His mother wanted Mike to complete Russian mission school so that he would not have to be a fisherman; her wish was for him to become a priest. Mike had interrupted his mother and told her he had enrolled himself in public school and wasn't going to be a priest, but planned to become a fisherman. His mother was about to strike Mike when his father intervened stating that the boy had a right to make his own choices for it was his life to plan. Mike felt a lot of animosity toward his mother for nothing seemed to suit her. Lately his father came to his defense on many occasions as Mike was learning to express his opinion and feelings and thoughts.

Mike spent many days at his secluded camp for here he could think and be on his own. It had become one of his favorite places in his young world. As he sat there gazing at the mountains of bright red, it reminded him of the strawberries his father and he planted several years before. Suddenly he was aware of the sound of breaking waves on the reef, bringing him back to the present. With a glance to the distant eastern sky, he saw that the blackish gray clouds released wet snow. The wind had picked up and Mike knew it would be on him in moments. No longer able to see the mainland from the sudden onslaught of the storm, he sped toward camp. He was thankful for its secure location, for it was well protected from the impending storm.

As he entered his camp, he was reaching for his rifle out of the lean-to when Kitty returned with a snowshoe rabbit. Kitty sat with it in his mouth for a moment, and then released the hare to the ground as an offering for Mike before retracing his steps into the woods.

Mike built up the fire with alder and cottonwood to make more coals for cooking. He carefully cleaned the animal and arranged it on the spit above the coals. As the rabbit cooked, he took the skin, scraped the fur off and stretched it between two

sticks placed into the ground to be dried by the fire. Soon Kitty returned with a second rabbit. He laid it at the edge of camp and ate it, as he did not care for cooked food except smoked salmon.

By the time their meal was at an end, the storm was in full glory, a true blizzard. The waves raised ten to fifteen feet high along the shoreline. The wind seemed to come from all directions. It would deposit ice on the cliffs as the salty spray made contact with the rocks.

Kitty found shelter under a fallen spruce tree. Mike crawled into his bed roll. It was made from two pieces of moose hide covered on the inside with cloth and stuffed with feathers. He laid there watching the flames flickering, dancing in the shadows, while hearing the storm winds blow. In the warm security of his lean-to he drifted off to a peaceful sleep.

It was early the next morning Kitty had awakened Mike by making a lot of noise. As Mike got up and dressed, Kitty took off. Mike was preparing to make tea, then thought he heard a scream, or was it the wind? Kitty returned to camp, very agitated and urging Mike to go with him. There was a thicket just a short distance away, and Mike could see Kitty had something there He went to investigate. About a hundred yards from his camp he found three lost children about his age, cold, crying and hungry. They had been in the storm all night, wet and confused for they couldn't find their way home.

Mike helped them back to his campsite one at a time for they had been in the elements too long to walk alone.

The storm had let up and the weather had warmed while the sun rose. Mike reassured the children, checked for frostbite, dried them and saw to it they were dressed warmly. He then secured them in his lean-to and stoked the fire. Mike was concerned for one of the boys who had blackened feet and part of his leg badly frostbitten as well, so he packed it in the snow. After feeding them smoked salmon, hardtack, and tea he informed them he was going to town for help.

Mike chose the shortest route, for he was concerned about the one boy's feet. It was understood that without knowledge of the wild harsh lands of Alaska, you should always have a guide and warm clothing and boots for the weather is bound to change. Those unable to find shelter suffer the consequences. He had hoped that this time he could help the boy retain his feet and be able to walk again.

Hiking at a fast pace through deep snow, Kitty traveling behind, he determined that going up and over the hill to the next bay was the quickest route. Following the stream lead to the next hill, then up and over again to the main bay that lead to the old sawmill. Knowing he had to reach the only road in the area he pushed at a quicker stride.

As he came to the top of the final hill he heard horns honking and saw many cars on the road. People were looking for the three young hikers that hadn't returned the night before. Mike rushed downhill to find Ed, a classmate of his and said, "They are at my camp. I found them this morning."

Ed had been to the camp several times before and knew its location, so he gathered a dozen men and led them to the children. Meanwhile, Mike was offered a ride to town, which he gladly accepted for the hike had not been easy. Kitty fell into a lope and went through the woods heading to his den under the tree root. By the time Mike arrived home, Kitty was fast asleep.

The following day Mike and Kitty had become heroes and the whole town knew of the storm-weathering youth who had conquered the elements and saved three of his peers who hadn't the knowledge of survival that Mike had.

Mike looked at his father in a respectful way and was thankful for the lessons and knowledge he had shared with him. Life experiences seem small to some and have great value to others.

FOUR

As spring approached, Kitty was getting very restless and irritable. He would go off into the woods days at a time as if in search of something. He would return more irritable than before. Kitty was going through changes a young Mike did not understand. His father tried to explain the changes, telling his son that Kitty needed to be with his own kind. He was aware of what might happen when they returned to the mainland, and wanted to prepare his son for Kitty's possibly leaving for good.

The preparations for the coming fishing season were underway. It was young Mike's responsibility to prepare the skiffs and as they were also going to gill net this year, he prepared the nets attaching the corks and lead to them. While he was working on the beach, Kitty would stay close but was very nervous. This concerned young Mike, and he wondered if he would be able to get Kitty on the boat, and about the close quarters for the long trip to camp.

As the preparations were completed and they began loading equipment on the boat and in the skiffs, Kitty stayed close. When they would finish for the day he would stay on the boat until their return in the morning. The loading took less time than Mike's father and Cappy thought, and when completed, it would still be about five days before they left for the fish camp. Young Mike asked if he could go to his special camp for a couple of days, but his father explained that when Kitty got into the deep woods, he might run off and not return in time.

When it was finally time to leave, though the lynx's attitude was disturbing, the decision was made to take Kitty along. The weather was still cold, and the route to the mainland was very hard. Traveling the water was rough, and winds high even in early May. A mixture of snow and rain was falling, the waves sprayed salty mists and the boat fought the sea over the 80 miles of open water to the bay where they would spend the summer.

The waves were breaking over the bow sending salt spray over everything. The boat

fought the sea, but as the men worked to control it, Kitty just sat in the bow or paced around the deck, seeming undisturbed.

Finally they entered the bay where calming waters greeted the beleaguered boat. It was still chilly, but calm. As they entered the cove, it was high tide, so they decided to wait an hour and beach the boat for unloading until low tide. That would give them about 10 hours to finish before the tide came back in. Kitty stood at the side of the boat looking at the water and the shore. Young Mike was afraid he would jump in and try to swim ashore. Mike's father told him not to worry even if he did, since lynx were good swimmers. Kitty held fast however, and finally lay down to wait.

When they finally beached the boat, the snow still lay on the ground. There was a chill in the air and the clouds hung low on the hills. Kitty, in a sudden giant leap, was on the beach, darting along the streambed and into the forest where he disappeared into the woods. Mike hoped he would return in a few days.

While they were unloading the gear, Mike noticed a look of concern on his father's and Cappy's faces. They had noticed a lot of bear sign around the camp and were worried since young Mike would be tending the gill nets, and cleaning and smoking the fish he caught. This would surely attract bears. After the supplies were removed from the boat and the camp re-established, the three of them built a larger smoke house. It was Mike's job to fillet and smoke fish and maintain the smoke house while the men fished. Another of his chores would be to keep it constantly stoked with firewood.

As the season got underway, it was hard and steady work, and no thought of Kitty was on Mike's mind for several weeks.

FIVE

⟶⟩●⟨⟶

As the summer months passed and the season was coming to an end, Mike became worried about Kitty; the leaves were turning color and you could feel the frost in the air. The setting sun would turn the bay into a golden mirror, and while daydreaming into it, Mike wondered if the lynx was going to be all right and if he would ever see him again.

That night after supper, Mike took the trash to the pit they had dug several years ago behind the tent. He dumped it in, poured diesel oil over it and burned, as they had done every night to keep bears away.

The next day they attached a pulley and rope to a tree, and using driftwood logs, pulled the two skiffs up near the camp. They stretched the nets out to dry as they loaded up the salmon and broke camp for the season's end.

As Mike was bundling smoked fish, he glanced over to the stream and noticed movement — it was Kitty. He was watching the men working at loading their catch for the year. Mike called, "Kitty!" and the lynx made a mewing sound; then a female with two small kittens appeared. As Mike started to approach, Kitty growled and the female and kittens disappeared into the brush. Mike took a salmon and tossed it to Kitty.

The lynx picked it up and vanished into the brush.

Mike watched him go as tears sprang to his eyes.

Though he didn't know it, he would not see Kitty

again for many years. His father, who had been

watching, put his hand on young Mike's shoulder

and said quietly, "Sometimes it's hard to say good bye to a close friend, Mike."

That night after supper, they took all the remaining trash to the pit and poured the remaining diesel over it. Once lit, it burned through the night. Next morning at daybreak, they covered the pit with dirt and Mike's father dug a spruce tree sapling and planted it in the middle of the mound. They took down the tent and loaded the boat for the trip to town. As they were rowing to the boat, Mike was in the bow of the skiff, looking toward shore. He started laughing and when his father asked what was so funny, he pointed to the campsite where two bears were walking around and sniffing. It was the only bears they had seen all summer.

The trip back to home was uneventful; the weather was calm and where it had taken nearly four days to reach camp, the return was less than two. Mike still wondered why they had him smoke so many salmon. When they docked in town he found out. His father and Cappy informed him that he was to sell them and that would be his pay for the season. They told him he should get between 25 and 50 cents a salmon. That would have amounted to what his share of the catch for the season would have been if he had worked the boat.

Ed, a friend of young Mike's, came to see if he had any smoked salmon to sell. Mike told him he had several hundred and what his father had told him to expect for them. Ed told Mike that all his sold almost before he could get it out of the smokehouse, and that they were selling for six dollars a salmon! Mike was thrilled. He put some aside for the family's winter use and sold the rest. He ended up making more money than both his father and Cappy combined.

In the few months they were gone, their little town had almost tripled in size. Mike was glad that Kitty stayed in the wild; he would have been caged up. School had started and one day when Mike came home, his father called him and said, "I want to take you trapping this year." Mike was silent for a few moments, then looked his father in the eyes and said, "No, I want to stay in school." Then, gathering his courage, he said he did not want to go trapping as he felt it was cruel. He stiffened himself in preparation for the tongue-lashing he felt was coming. Instead, his father just put his hand on his shoulder and said, "That is fine, son;

there will be a lot of ways to make a living. As your lynx had to make a choice of two worlds, he chose the one best for him. You are a man now and will have to make your own choices as well."

Mike was relieved by his father's understanding attitude, not realizing it would be about the last conversation they would ever have. Big Mike and his trapping partner Ray left the next day for the season and never returned. An air and sea search was made, and it was learned that they were in a port about the middle of December. The weather was rough but they had decided to return home anyway. They were never seen again. It was presumed they were lost at sea.

As time passed, Mike finished school, got a job and still spent time in his camp — alone with memories of Kitty and his father.

SIX

—————➤●◄—————

As the years passed, Mike thought of Kitty often. He had never returned to the camp after the loss of his father. The important thing that he remembered was that a man of few words has an increased chance at wisdom. Mike missed the companionship of both the father and the lynx.

Mike grew to young manhood, and when the Korean war broke out, joined the Air Force. He applied for Officer's Candidate School and flight training and was accepted for both. While in flight training, Mike met a young lady that had already received her wings. Her name was Marilynn. They began dating and she was enthusiastic about Mike's stories of his and Kitty's adventures. After a few months, she was transferred but they kept in touch.

At the end of basic flight training Mike was told he could go on to advance training or to flight engineering and navigator's school. Mike decided on the school, not quite sure why. Upon completion, he was assigned to a MATS squadron in the state of Washington. He picked up his first assignment for the next day with the plane number and crew members, and to his surprise and delight, Marilynn was the pilot. They met at the briefing and as they were walking across the ramp to the plane, Mike noticed she had a mischievous look — like the cat that has swallowed the canary. He soon saw why. Marilynn pointed out the plane, and what Mike saw brought a lump to his throat and tears to his eyes. On the nose of the plane was painted a picture of a large lynx with the word "Kitty" over the top. Speechless, Mike turned to Marilynn for a spontaneous, warm embrace.

Time passed, and as the Korean War was coming to a close, Mike and Marilynn became engaged. When the war ended, Mike took his discharge, while Marilynn decided to stay in for another year. As Mike headed back to his home town, he stopped at a private flying school and received his commercial pilot's license. On return home, he talked to longtime friend Bob, who had given him his first flying lessons and had a growing flight business. He gave Mike a flight test and a job.

Mike received a letter from Marilynn that she was going to get her discharge and come to Alaska. Mike was excited but also apprehensive, as he was receiving a lot of flak from his mother — about his flying airplanes instead of fishing and following his native culture and especially his decision to marry a non-native. One day, Mike's half-sister spoke up and said, "Well, Mother, you married a non-native!" That only made things worse.

That afternoon, Mike met with George, an old friend of his father's, who ran a boat for the cannery. George told Mike they were going to make a quick trip to the cove and asked if he'd like to go along. Mike agreed, and they headed out. The next day as they came into open water between the island and the cove, it was calm. The sun was shining brightly and Mike noticed some porpoise playing in front of the boat.

This always fascinated him; the way they would swim with their tails just inches from the bow. The porpoise in these waters looked more like a miniature Orca or killer whale. They had a long sharp dorsal fin that looked like the blade of a two-edged broadsword. Their markings were similar; dark body with white underbelly, and white spots on the cheeks.

As they came to the cove the skiff was lowered for Mike and alone, he rowed for shore. Beaching and securing the skiff, he saw that the tent frame had collapsed. The old skiffs were deteriorating; one was almost completely rotted away. As he walked around, he saw a red fox with a rodent in its mouth scamper under the skiff, and he thought perhaps it was being used as a den. Mike wouldn't disturb it to find out.

Filled with nostalgia, Mike went over and sat on the log that he and Kitty had shared so many years before. He glanced over toward the stream and spotted an old lynx peering out and sniffing the air. Mike was stunned for a moment, and then said, "Is that you, Kitty?" The lynx's ears perked up and he began walking slowly toward Mike. He was dragging a hind leg and Mike realized he was badly hurt. The lynx came up to Mike and sniffed him, and then put his massive front paws on Mike's leg and cradled his chin in Mike's lap. Deeply moved, Mike stroked Kitty's ears and could see that he had been shot. There was no exit wound. Mike thought that Kitty, being used to humans, may have seen some near the camp and tried to approach them when they shot at him.

As Mike lovingly stroked Kitty's ears, he suddenly realized that life had left his beloved lynx. Deeply grieved, but grateful for this last moment, he wrapped the cat in his jacket. Looking around, he found an old pickax and shovel under the floor of the tent site. They were rusty but useable.

He dug a hole and buried Kitty, piling rocks on top so nothing would disturb his dear old friend and childhood companion.

Sitting by the cairn, Mike heard the whistle of the returning boat and knew it was time to leave. As he rowed to the boat he looked back and saw a young lynx by the log. He knew Kitty would live on through his offspring.

The trip back to town was smooth. When they arrived, Mike learned that Marilynn had flown in the day before. They met and went to a restaurant for lunch. He told her about Kitty and tears came to her eyes. She told Mike she had gone to the office looking for him, introduced herself to Bob, and that he had offered her a job since two pilots had quit to return to the lower 48.

Mike began to explain his mother's attitude, but
Marilynn told him she had met her the day before.
She won Mike's mother over, they had had dinner
together and she spent the night there.

As the couple made arrangements for the wedding, Marilynn stayed with Mike's half-sister. Mike had been astonished at his mother's change of attitude, but the biggest surprise was when his mother asked if she could make Marilynn's wedding dress! Mike knew she was a fine seamstress, and had seen her make several dresses before. They couldn't get the material in their small town in time for the wedding, but Marilynn told Mike that Bob said she could have a plane to fly his mother and half-sister to a large town on the mainland. Amazed, Mike said he had offered to give his mother a plane ride several times and she wouldn't get near one of those "contraptions." She said that if God wanted people to fly he would have given them wings. Mike jokingly told his mother God must have given him wings but not attached, because he flies.

The next day Marilynn flew the women to the city for shopping: his mother's first and only time in an airplane. After their return and when the dress was finished, Mike and Marilynn were married in the Russian Orthodox Church. In the years following, they both flew for Bob and as time went by, had two children — a boy and girl. Mike's mother passed away shortly after the girl was born.

The years seemed to slip by. The children were now nine and ten. The day before their twelfth wedding anniversary, they were in the office talking to Bob. Mike mentioned how he had always wanted to take Marilynn and his children to the cove, and Bob suggested they take a plane and fly up in the morning. It was to be his anniversary present to them.

The family took off at daybreak the next morning and headed for the cove. As they started over the open stretch of water, Mike thought of the last time he had made that trip with Kitty. It had taken over four days and this one would be just over an hour. They landed and taxied the plane up onto the beach, then got out and started walking around. Mike pointed out the skiffs that were now completely deteriorated. Then he noticed and pointed out the tree that his father had planted years ago over the trash mound. It had grown tall and strong. The kids picked wildflowers and put them on Kitty's grave, and the four of them spent several hours wading in the stream and walking barefoot on the sandy beach.

As they were walking toward the plane to return to town, they heard a noise. Looking back, they saw two adult lynx and two kittens sitting on the old log. Marilynn and Mike looked at each other and their children and laughed delightedly.

They took off and as the plane lifted gently into the air, Mike looked over at his wife sitting in the co-pilot's seat. Looking into those deep blue, smiling eyes, the words of his father came back to him: he knew, that as with Kitty, he had made a choice between two worlds — and also like Kitty, the one he made was the best one for him. As she returned Mike's gaze, Marilynn reached over and squeezed his hand. The spiritual bond between them grew even stronger, and though many more years would pass, it would never diminish or be broken, even by death.

Printed in the United States
63823LVS00002B/13-18